A SENSE OF OCCASION

'Woodcraft's take on growing up mod in Chelmsford is poignant, heart-warming and hip. She gets to the essence of what it's like to be a young woman who knows the difference between the A-side and the B-side and how that might matter.' Val Wilmer, author of *As Serious as Your Life* and *Mama Said There'd Be Days Like This*

'What a writer Woodcraft is! This brilliant collection is an irresistible page-turner. The inter-connected stories about Linda and her best friend Sandra, about Marie and her bridesmaids, and about the local hero Mick Flynn create a very special magic.' Sue Katz, author of *Lillian's Last Affair*

Elizabeth Woodcraft was born and grew up on a council estate in Chelmsford. She became a mod at 13 and took her suede coat to Birmingham University. Later she trained as a teacher and taught English in Leicester and Tours in France. She then moved to London where she worked for Women's Aid, the organisation which supports women who suffer domestic violence. Her experiences there led her to become a barrister.

Elizabeth Woodcraft has also published two crime novels, featuring barrister Frankie Richmond – Good Bad Woman and Babyface. Good Bad Woman was shortlisted for the John Creasey Award for Best First Crime Novel, and in the US won the Lambda Literary Award.

She lives in London with her partner.

Contact her on www.elizabethwoodcraft.com
Follow her on Twitter @lizwoodcraft

ELIZABETH WOODCRAFT

A SENSE OF OCCASION

The Chelmsford Stories

Ladder Press

Published by Ladder Press

theladderpress@gmail.com

For Christine Wallace

the best friend I could ever have had

and much better than I deserved

ACKNOWLEDGEMENTS

My thanks go to the following:

Maureen Hanscomb for her painstaking work, proof reading the stories and for pointing out the inconsistencies, but also the parts that made her laugh. Any mistakes are mine.

Christine Wilkinson for the most wonderful cover design and her patience as I changed my mind so often. And for making a Betty Crocker cake with me.

To all the people who over the years have listened to the stories, in classes and in writing groups and given me their feedback and support including Iris Ansell, Dorothy Reinders, Penelope Overton and John Petherbridge. To Bill Greensmith for just enjoying the stories and reminding me how to spell Ben Sherman. To Roy Kelly for keeping me writing.

To all the mods in Chelmsford who made life in the Sixties so exciting and so much fun, particularly Mick Flynn, whose story is only partly told here, mixed in with some poetic licence, that he and his wife Ann knew all about.

And as ever my greatest thanks to Caroline Spry, for her love, confidence and encouragement, without which, none of this would be possible.

CONTENTS

TEA FOR TOMMY

On the table is a plate of marshmallows in striped red and silver paper. There are small half-empty jars of Robertson's jam, strawberry, blackcurrant and marmalade. There is a plate of sliced white Wonderloaf which my mum made me spread with butter because it's my fault he's here and the bread has holes in because I can't spread butter very well. On two saucers are sliced banana and sliced apple and in front of each of us is a fifth of Vesta Beef Curry for two which mum has padded out with extra rice and more raisins. Which I hate.

My sister Judith is wearing Wellingtons on purpose and is showing off, pretending people like him come to our house for tea every day.

My mum has put on the American apron that her penfriend Mildred sent her. It has the pleats ironed in and I am going to have it when I grow up. Mum won't sit down yet because she's making the tea in the kitchen. He said he would love a cup of tea with two sugars. I can hear her slinging a spoon into the saucer of the best cups. She's ashamed that there's not enough to eat but angry at feeling ashamed. And she'd been meaning to have a new perm.

I cannot believe that Tommy Steele is really sitting round our table in our living room. The table hides the bare patch in the middle of the carpet so that's all right and mum did the ironing last night so there aren't piles of washing everywhere.

And here he is. He looks just like he did in 'The Duke Wore Jeans', really smiling. I wish my best friend Sandra was here to see him, but I'm glad my dad isn't because I know he'd laugh at him. He'd laugh at me too, for the letter I wrote to Tommy's fan club saying my biggest wish in the world was for Tommy to come to my house. Only if he was coming to Chelmsford to do a show of course, I wouldn't expect him to come specially. And because my mum makes really delicious cakes. Which she does, except they are usually made from Viota mix, although the other day, unexpectedly because they're very expensive, she made a Betty Crocker cake which was lovely. Which was the day I wrote the letter. And drew a picture of the cake. And said I was 15.

And then just this afternoon the phone rang and it was Tommy's agent, who said Tommy was coming to do a show in Witham and could he stop off and have tea with us and we could have four tickets to the show. I couldn't believe it because Witham is so horrible. Mum wasn't in from work and my dad was going to a meeting so I just said yes.

Of course the sky fell later. I had to hoover the stairs. Judith had to dust the mantelpiece because mum said she was as much to blame, because should have stopped me. Then we had to tidy our bedroom even though I said he wouldn't go upstairs. She said he'd have to go to the toilet, which I felt was unnecessary to point out, since he's famous. Then I had to go down the shops to buy a large tin of spaghetti or a Vesta Beef Curry, and even though they had the spaghetti I didn't get it because I didn't want Tommy thinking we hadn't made an effort. I knew he'd want something different. For all I knew he'd never had curry before. I wanted his evening in Chelmsford to be an evening to remember.

I am wearing my new blue flowery skirt with the elastic waist but I wish I hadn't put on this T-shirt because the stripes don't go with the skirt and it's not mine anyway.

I say to him, 'Have you been to Chelmsford before? I've got 12 pictures of you,' and then want to die with shame because I haven't and what if he asks to see them? I'll say they're over Sandra's. I say quickly, 'I know all the words to "Nairobi"' and I sing, 'Give a little yoohoo, yoohoo!' and Judith says, 'Linda.'

Tommy is wearing jeans so I'm glad he's come to our house and not Sandra's because her dad thinks jeans are disgusting. Tommy is sitting on our chairs and I am praying he stops tipping the seat back by the time mum comes back in with his tea. He talks funny, with a sort of drawl and he's very interested in hearing what my sister did at school today. When I go and stand at the French windows to show him the actions that Sandra and I do when we sing "Butterfingers" he hardly even looks at me.

Judith likes him. She's always told me she doesn't but she's really talking to him now. She's telling him about being a teenager, which she has been for precisely two months. She's smiling at him. She says, 'I loved you in 'The Duke Wore Jeans' which is a big lie, she never even saw it. She only knows what happened because I told her, after I'd been with Sandra and her mum and we walked so far along the row that I sat in the fire bucket by mistake. And she only listened when I told her about it because she liked the sound of June Laverick's dress.

But now Tommy is going out to the kitchen. He's saying something to my mum. I hear her answer. Then I hear her laugh.

Judith, who has been pulling her left Wellington on and off in triumph, stops and looks at me. We are not used to the sound of mum laughing.

He is saying, 'My nan still lives there, and my mum lives just round the corner, near Bacon School.'

Mum's voice is too low to make out what she's saying and then Tommy says 'something something Girls Life Brigade.' I can't believe he's talking about anything so boring. Mum is always going on about the GLB. Then there is a crash.

Judith and I look at each other, our eyes wide with panic. This is it – I'll never be allowed out to play ever again. Judith hisses urgently at me, 'Don't go out there,' but I'm only going to look, I'm not going to say anything. I slide into the hall and peep through the crack in the kitchen door.

My mum is leaning with her back against the sink. There are pieces of china and spilt tea all over the floor. Tommy is standing beside my mum. He's got his arm round her. He's stroking her hair. As I watch, frozen with outrage, he leans forward and kisses her cheek. How dare she?

THE OTHER ALDERMASTON MARCH

We had hot cross buns on Good Friday and Easter Eggs on Easter Sunday. The Bradys had enormous Easter Eggs but they never had hot cross buns. They were Catholic, so it could have been that they didn't want to eat the cross, especially on a Friday. They didn't eat meat on Fridays, they had fish and chips. But they weren't that religious. They never went to church.

My mum was more religious than they were. As

7

a result I wasn't allowed out to play on Sundays and I had to go to Sunday School. It was a miracle I was allowed out today, being Good Friday. But mum had other things on her mind, and my dad didn't care about the religious significance of any day-off.

Sandra Brady and I had been best friends since my family had moved onto the estate in 1952, eight years before, when I was three. Sandra was a couple of years older than me. Ours was a new estate built a few years after the war. Sandra lived across the road. We had a phone before they did, but as soon as Sandra's phone was installed we rang each other and opened our front doors to watch each other speaking.

We played together in our gardens, put on shows for the other kids in the street and produced a newspaper for the houses round about. She came on our Sunday School outings to Walton-on-the-Naze.

Today we were helping Mr Brady re-paper Sandra's bedroom, which she shared with her older sister Marie. We were scraping the wallpaper off the wall by the window. Sandra and I each had a small metal trowel. She was doing the side near Marie's bed, and I was doing Sandra's side, in case I did something wrong.

8

We had the light on because the day was so dark and it was raining.

My arm was getting tired. 'What's the time?' I said. Then, because I didn't want to seem bored or rude, I added, 'My dad's cooking our dinner today.'

Mr Brady was up the ladder scraping off the old frieze over the window. 'Where's your mum, then?' he asked.

'I'm not sure,' I said, though I did know where she was. She was on the Aldermaston march. Only not from Aldermaston this year, because this Easter there was another march in Essex, starting from Wethersfield, the American airbase. My mum had gone with the Chelmsford Campaign for Nuclear Disarmament group, in cars, the Grenvilles, Beryl and Jeremy Husband, the Van Gazen family, who dad called the Vagrants, and Ken and Robert Sadd from Witham. I didn't want to say Campaign for Nuclear Disarmament or even CND, because Mr Brady would ask me what it stood for, and it would sound posh, like I was showing off. 'Big words for a little girl,' he'd say.

I looked out of the window, thinking about the march, wondering if mum was very wet but almost certain her feet would be dry. She was wearing her new shoes. She'd wanted sensible walking shoes, but didn't know where to buy them. She'd ended up with a pair of round-toed, ruby-brown lace-ups which looked heavy and ugly. Mum said they were really uncomfortable. By now she probably had about six plasters on her feet. And that plastic rain-hat on her head that Mrs Brady sniggered about.

On the march they were probably singing - something like 'Ban ban ban the bloody H-bomb.' My mum swearing! Singing and swearing! I knew the songs because mum had a CND song book, with the music in it, and sometimes I would go into the front room and try to sing them on my own. Mum was probably changing the words and singing 'Ban Ban Ban the blinking H-bomb.'

I knew a lot about the H-bomb, and the A-bomb which fell on Hiroshima on the 6th August 1945 and then Nagasaki, because we had books about them in the bookcase in the front room. Sometimes, on Sundays particularly, when we came back from Sunday School I would sit on the settee, and read about the bomb, the noise, the flash, the people falling in the streets, the outline of their bodies left on the ground, how some seemed all right and then when they were touched their skin came off like gloves. I wanted to ban the H-bomb. I wanted to go on the march but mum said we couldn't go till we were 12 because she didn't want people saying she'd indoctrinated us.

I'd read more about Hiroshima and Nagasaki than I had about the Blitz. The only thing I really knew about the Blitz was what happened to my mum in the air-raid in 1940. Mum was 16. Her brothers were all away in the war. Mum and her sisters and their mum and dad went to their Auntie Hilda's in Woodford one night for a bath. They had to go, because Leytonstone, where they lived, had been bombed and the water mains had been blown up so there was no running water, but Woodford was quiet and they still had all their pipes.

That night the girls had their baths, as usual all using the same water which got cold and grey and cloudy with soap and dirt, then their mum, and lastly their dad. Then they got ready for bed. Everyone slept downstairs during the Blitz, even in Woodford, just in case. Their dad got the settee in the scullery. All the others were in the living room. Their mum said as a treat, Vera, my mum, could sleep on the settee with her, but Vera said, no, she wanted the armchairs. So their mum and their sister Honor, the oldest girl, took the settee. They all settled down, the others moaning about the mattresses on the hard floor and Vera getting the chairs, and their Auntie Hilda switched off the light. They all fell asleep.

At about two in the morning the bomb dropped. Just one in Woodford. Nobody knew why, if it was a young inexperienced bomber, who just missed the railway lines, or a pilot who thought it would do less harm here than in the centre. It was a direct hit and the house fell down on top of them all. They had to be dug out. The ARP people had been told that there was only an old lady living there, but girls kept coming out, Vera, Rita, Sheila, Iris, Beryl, all dusty and dazed in their nighties. And then they heaved away blocks of stone and lumps of metal and pulled out the bodies, Auntie Hilda, their father and their sister Honor. Lastly the ARP men brought out their mother, moving her gently from the settee. She was alive and scarcely a mark on her, but she died the next day.

But in our house we didn't really talk about it, what it felt like for them, lying in all the rubble, looking at the sky, then everyone watching as they staggered out of the house. Suddenly being orphans, and all split up, and then how they were given somewhere to live together in Chelmsford. And there was no anger, we didn't hate the Germans. It was war. It happened. But we didn't like the Americans because they used the A-bomb in Japan and that wasn't necessary.

Not all Americans of course - my mum had an American pen-friend, Mildred, and we liked her. She sent us presents at Christmas and big thick rolls of magazines, McCalls, Women's Day, where I read stories about egg-nog, and girls with ear muffs and flying hair ice-skating on frozen lakes.

I put down my trowel and went home. We were having tinned potatoes, tinned peas, tinned carrots, and Fray Bentos steak and kidney pie, cut equally into four, with gravy. It was lovely. Especially the gravy. We were saving the other quarter of the dinner for mum. We never had tinned things normally, except for afters. Mum loved tinned fruit, especially pineapple, because they couldn't have it in the war. I hated it, all tinny and slimy and cold, and then evaporated milk on top. It was only nice when we had cream. We had Fussels, and we were allowed one and a half teaspoons each. But today dad had done tinned steamed sponge pudding and custard. 'Give me a tin opener and I will give you a high class repast,' he said.

After dinner, my sister Judith, me and dad went up to the Angel, the pub right by our school, to watch the march go past and wave at mum. It was a surprise.

We were standing outside the pub. We had been there for ages and we were soaking wet. We were wearing our coats because we didn't have macs and we didn't have umbrellas, no-one in our street had umbrellas. Dad was smoking – 'You get more out of life with a Kensitas'. It was all right for him, he had his trilby, which was so covered in hair oil that it was waterproof. I had my school hat on - the knitted, pony-tail hat, and rain was dribbling off the pony-tail, down the back of my neck. I thought, mum will go mad when she sees us, standing here all wet.

There was a straggle of other people standing across the way, who kept stepping into the road to look down the hill. They were dad's union members. When we'd arrived, dad said, 'Wha'cheer' to them, in his old-fashioned way, and made us say hello.

Someone said, 'Here they come.' Dad threw his cigarette away.

The first thing we saw was a wet sagging banner that said, 'Wethersfield to London, Easter 1960' with a CND symbol painted on it. It wasn't a really big march like the Aldermaston ones on telly, it didn't go all the way across the street, but it was long enough that we couldn't see the end. When the marchers saw us they shouted, 'Ban the Bomb. Join the march.' We clapped and I wanted to shout, but I was swallowing.

We were looking for mum. Judith saw her first, she was carrying one of the poles for the Chelmsford banner. We all waved and shouted 'Mum'. She looked over at us and raised her eyebrows. That meant, 'Look at me, I'm drenched. There's a rip in my plastic mac and this banner is really heavy.' Then she shook her head because she saw that we were wet. Then she grinned which meant, 'It's nice of you to come. See you later.'

Judith and I were very proud. We knew this was the right view to have about the bomb. Next year Judith would be 12 and she'd be able to go on the march. I did want the bomb to be banned but I hoped that it wouldn't be till after Easter 1963, so I'd have been on at least one. I knew that was wrong, but I just hoped it to myself. I certainly wouldn't pray for it. But then I wouldn't pray for the bomb to be banned at all, because that would obviously be a waste of time. If God had any power over it, why had he let it be dropped in the first place?

I was going to have my tea over at Sandra's. When I got over there they'd finished the bedroom, they'd even put up the new frieze over the window, pink and yellow waves, and Mr Brady was very pleased, although Sandra said the Pollyfilla took a little while to dry where I'd made a dent in the wall. We had fish and chips.

Mrs Brady was cutting up the apple pie when the news comes on the television. I was hoping they wouldn't show the march. But they did. On the screen it was raining and everyone was wet. I looked for my mum but thankfully I couldn't see her.

'Bleeding hell,' Sandra's mum said, pointing at the television with the knife. 'The state of that and the price of fish. And they're all communists.'

'That's Linda's mum,' Sandra said.

'Oh,' her mum said, and looked at me and burst out laughing.

I went hot. I knew her brother had died in the war. I knew they voted Labour. And I knew they always paid for me to go on the Dodgems when we went to Ipswich. But she didn't know what she was talking about.

Mr Brady said, 'Now then.'

Sandra said, 'Here, Linda.' She pushed the pink glass bowl of cream towards me. The bowl was full, the cream stood up in thick, glossy peaks. It must have been a big tin.

'How many spoonfuls can I have?' As soon as I said it, I knew it was wrong, and stupid and revealing.

'Dear oh dear,' said Mrs Brady. 'You can have as much as you like.' And I knew she was thinking communists may have big ideas but they haven't got any money. They go to church and go on marches but they wear torn plastic macs.

I took a teaspoon and a half.

'Have more than that,' Mrs Brady said.

'Thank you, that's all I want,' I said.

BILL'S BIG MOMENT

Mr and Mrs Brady were sitting in the living room. It was half past seven and still light, but the curtains were drawn so the sun wouldn't interfere with the picture on the TV screen. They hadn't had their tea yet. The idea was that Marie should make the tea, in order to impress her new chap Bill. Sandra, their other daughter, was over the road having tea with her friend Linda, in case she made any clever remarks. But Marie and Bill weren't home yet.

It had been their dad's suggestion that Marie

should cook tonight, to let Bill know that she could prepare a decent meal. Marie wouldn't have minded but her mum and dad didn't know Bill at all. Bill didn't care whether he ate cardboard with shaving cream, he only really cared about his car.

When Marie opened the back door and led Bill into the kitchen, she called immediately, 'Sorry we're late, the bus didn't come.'

She hadn't planned on them coming on the bus. They were supposed to have roared up the road triumphantly in the Mini. The Mini was, in fact, one of the reasons she liked Bill. And she knew it would impress her dad.

But tonight the Mini was in the garage. Bill was having leather racing seats fitted.

They'd arranged to meet at twenty past six at the shop, which was later than she normally left, but they were checking in the new autumn range of Ladies' Outerwear.

She hadn't wanted to work in a shop, she'd stayed on at school to do typing and shorthand, but she'd got bored with it. She and her mate Deirdre had more fun going to the Youth Clubs on the estates in town. Then Deirdre moved away and Marie failed her exams.

But the shop wasn't bad, because it was quite upmarket and she didn't really mind staying late because some ice-blue macs had just come in, that would look nice with a tartan scarf and she was hoping to put one by. She liked working with the different fabrics and the colours. Bill liked blue, he had once commented on her twin-set, saying 'I like that blue,' so she had worn it to work today specially, even though it was a bit impractical, being so pale.

As she walked out of the shop, she draped the cardigan round her shoulders and fastened it with one button at the neck. Bill was leaning against the wall of the bookies' across the road. He was wearing a pale blue Ben Sherman shirt and grey slacks. As she reached him he pulled himself upright and looked her up and down, frowning. 'Why are you wearing that jumper? That blue?' he said. 'It's the same as mine. We look like a couple of prats.'

'I'll change it when we get home,' she said, her heart pounding. 'It was just for work.'

Walking through the town, up to the bus station, he kept flexing his hands. He'd bought a pair of driving gloves in readiness for the new car seats. The gloves were thick, brown leather and he was wearing them in. 'You have to weather them first,' he said, 'or the rain spoils them.' It wasn't raining. It was July. It wasn't even cold. They looked really big on his hands, and the seams stuck out, like the first draft of Frankenstein's monster. They made Marie feel a bit sick. She hoped he wouldn't keep them on in the house.

As they walked into the kitchen she could hear the Coronation Street theme music. She looked at her watch. Seven thirty. She sighed. It was just beginning.

If they'd had the car they'd have arrived at least half an hour earlier. They might have finished their tea by now, they'd certainly have got the introductions over with. Now her mum and dad wouldn't know what to do. Politeness would make them turn the sound down and smile at Bill, but their gaze would keep flickering back to the TV screen.

She smiled encouragingly at Bill and they went through the arch, into the living room. 'Mum, Dad, this is Bill.'

Her dad stood up and hesitated between the TV set and Bill. He glanced at Bill's outstretched hand. Bill gave a small laugh, almost embarrassed, and pulled off the gloves. Solemnly they shook hands. Mrs Brady, her eyes darting from the gloves to the screen, leaned across to the television and turned down the volume. She nodded at Bill.

There were only two comfortable chairs in the room, the TV chairs. Yellow and black with no arms, they were meant to match the contemporary wallpaper. Her mum and dad were sitting on them and made no attempt to move. Awkwardly Marie pointed to a hard chair and said to Bill, 'Sit down. I'll make some tea.'

She slipped back into the kitchen and switched on the kettle, straining to hear sounds of conversation from the living room. She heard nothing but the low hum of chat in the Rovers Return.

She lit the oven for the chops, turned on the gas under the potatoes and opened a tin of processed peas. While the kettle was boiling she ran upstairs to put on her red blouse.

She put two teabags into the stainless steel teapot and made the tea. She poured her mum and dad's out first because they liked it weak. Bill liked his strong. She didn't know what she liked, she supposed she was just one of those 'any way it comes' people. She carefully added a level spoonful of sugar to Bill's cup and stirred it, lovingly. Did she love him? She didn't know. Did he love her?

He ought to love her. She tried her best. She wore her thick dark hair in flick-ups, a style that took a lot of maintaining - she slept in painful rollers every night. Her face was small and heart shaped, with lips that looked almost like the mouths in her magazine, Romeo. Johnny Brown had said she was the prettiest girl at the Youth Club and then he'd asked her out. And she went, but when she brought him home her mum and dad had gone mad because he was wearing jeans and his hair was slicked back with grease. He worked in the greengrocer's and lived in one of the flats over the shops. Her dad said he was common and his mother was no better than she should be, not married and no father for Johnny. They hadn't gone out after that but when she walked past the shop he'd grin at her, and muck about, juggling with the oranges, or balancing a cabbage on his forehead.

The girls at the Youth Club thought Bill was a much better catch than Johnny. He was taller and earned more. And he had the Mini. It was nice having someone waiting for her after work, sitting in the car outside the shop. When she came out with the others she could just say 'Bye' and laughingly climb into the passenger seat. And sometimes he made cracks about people that made her laugh. He said her boss Mrs Freeman was a lazy cow, and George, the chap who ran the Youth Club was a ponce. She'd never dare say those things, but she did think them sometimes.

And he respected her, which was certainly important to her mum and dad. He didn't go too far. In fact, she would have liked him to be a bit more pushy, because she knew full well he'd gone all the way with other girls because he'd told her, but he said those girls were tarts, and she wasn't like that. His words had thrilled and appalled her at the same time. That she was different, better, someone he prized, was wonderful, and yet she felt it wasn't quite right, like he was keeping her in a box. It wasn't that she was cheap but she wanted something more.

The time she'd been to the pictures with Johnny they'd climbed up to the back row, just as the lights went down and he'd put his arm round her straight away, and in the boring bits of the film he'd kissed her, exploring her mouth with his tongue, holding her neck with his hand, his eyes glittering in the dark as he looked at her. She'd loved that.

She hadn't ever felt like that with Bill, specially not in the car, because he was really too tall for a Mini, leaning across the gear stick to kiss her a hard, bruising goodnight.

She put the cups on a tray and carried them into the living room. There was total silence. They were all watching Coronation Street. Suddenly all three burst out laughing. Bill was open mouthed, guffawing. 'Minnie Caldwell,' he snorted, wiping his eyes.

'It's the cat that got me,' her dad chuckled. 'What's its name?'

'Bobby,' they both said together, and started roaring again.

She put down the tray and went back out to the kitchen. Then the end-of-part-one music came on and the living room filled with conversation.

Marie turned down the gas under the potatoes and leaned against the sink.

In the living room Bill and Mr Brady were discussing cars. Even her mum joined in once or twice, to remind her dad of a car they'd nearly bought, or the name of a garage that had taken advantage.

I might as well not even be here! Marie thought. Who's he come to see? Me or them? She blew her nose.

When she carried the meal in, they were talking about motor accessories. Bill pulled his gloves out of his back pocket. Marie tried to hand him his plate but he was putting the gloves on again. He flexed his hands. Marie looked at Mr Brady, but he was smiling. She stood, waiting, with the chops cooling on the tray, while Mr and Mrs Brady touched the gloves and said how soft the leather was.

They ate with their plates on their laps, her dad and Bill chatting like old friends. Marie sat on the opposite side of the room, on the other hard chair, miserably chewing her food. They sat through the evening's programmes - World in Action, Police 5, the News.

At the next advert break Bill started the story about being stopped by the police because of his hub-caps. She said to him. 'Do you want to come and help me make another cup of tea?'

'No, you're all right.'

Her dad said, 'Bill's in the middle of a story here.'

She went out to the kitchen and heard her parents laugh when he got to the punch line that all they'd stopped him for was to find out where he'd got the hub-caps from.

She gripped the handle of the kettle. Suddenly, she was consumed with hatred for Bill. How could it be so easy for him? Them being so friendly, so interested. What was it? They were treating him as if he was an adult, as if he was something. They were showing him respect.

She opened the back door and went round the side of the house and out to the front garden. The daylight was fading and the street lights glowed weakly. She sat on the garden wall, willing Bill to notice her absence and come out and sit with her. They could hold hands, talk softly about the neighbours' gardens, maybe kiss.

Across the road the shops were in darkness, but above them the lights in the flats shone orange and friendly. She looked for Johnny's flat - second floor. For Johnny's room - third window along. Yes, the light was on. He was there. She could go up now and knock on the door and ask him if he wanted a cup of tea. You could bet your life he'd say yes. He wouldn't turn it down, whatever her mum and dad said. She had half a mind to do it. Why not?

She thought about it. What kind of idiot would she look knocking on the door asking for Johnny? For all she knew he'd got himself a proper girlfriend by now, probably that new girl who'd just started coming to the Youth Club. She wore really tight sweaters and Marie could imagine he'd like that.

'What's a nice girl like you doing on a wall like this?'

She turned sharply and nearly laughed out loud. It was Johnny. 'You made me jump!' she said.

'I'm just going up to the Prince of Orange for a drink,' he said. 'Do you want to come?'

'I can't. I'm – we're entertaining, we've got company.'

'And that's why you're sitting out here on your tod, is it?'

She sighed.

'Do you want to go out again, sometime?' he said.

She looked at him. His eyes glittered in the dusk.

'I can't.' She stood up.

'Your loss.' He shrugged. 'See you then.' He turned away.

'Is that it?' she said in a low voice.

He stopped. 'What?'

'Aren't you going to say anything else?'

'What do you want me to say? "Marie, I love you, come out with me"?'

'No…. maybe. I dunno.'

'All right. Marie, I think you're lovely, will you come out with me?'

'I can't.'

'Funny girl,' he said. 'Well, you know where I am.' He brushed her face with his finger and walked away, up the road.

As she went back into the kitchen she felt hot and excited.

The kettle had boiled. Tea! What was she doing making tea? She wanted to go outside, on her own, with - with Bill, stroll with him in the fading daylight, up to the bus stop. She needed him to put his arms round her, pull her to him, kiss her.

She carried the tea back into the living room. 'You'd better drink that quick, or the bus'll be up.'

'You've got bags of time,' her dad said. 'It'll only take you a minute to get up to the bus stop.'

Bill didn't seem anxious to move. 'Can I have a biscuit?' he said.

'I think I just heard the bus,' she said desperately. 'You mustn't be late home, Bill, your mum'll worry.'

Her dad looked at his watch. Reluctantly, they all stood up. 'Very nice to meet you, Mr and Mrs Brady,' Bill said.

'Nice to meet you too, son.' Her dad stretched to put his hand on Bill's shoulder. 'She may not be the brightest girl in the world, but you could do worse.'

'Oh Dad.' Marie cringed.

Bill grinned broadly. 'We've all got to go sometime.'

He and Mr Brady laughed.

Marie looked at her watch. 'The bus really will go soon,' she said.

'I'll just write down the name of that oil, for your car,' Mr Brady said. 'You only need a drop.' He searched the drawer where they kept the paper bags and bits of old string for a piece of paper.

At last Bill and Marie walked up the road. The bus was already waiting, purring gently, its lights glowing in the twilight. The conductor was sitting inside the bus. He leaned forward salaciously. 'You've got two minutes.'

'Where are my gloves?' Bill said. He patted his chest, poking into his breast pocket. He felt the sides of his trousers, jingling his pockets. The engine revved and the conductor stood up.

'Where are my fucking gloves?' Bill shouted.

'Did you leave... ? I think I saw them on the chair,' she said.

'Silly cow, why didn't you say something?'

The conductor rang the bell.

'Shall I go back and get them?'

'No, it's too late now. You can fucking well drop them off at my office tomorrow morning.'

The bus lurched and Bill jumped onto the platform. With a cloud of exhaust fumes the bus pulled away, and swayed down the road.

He was gone. Not a kiss, not a cuddle, no pressing her body into his. Not even an arrangement to meet again.

When she walked back into the house the fluorescent light was on in the kitchen and her dad was rinsing the cups.

'Very nice bloke that. He left his gloves behind.'

'I know,' she said.

'And you, sulking all night.'

'I couldn't get a word in.'

'You want to be careful. You might not get another chance with a chap like Bill,' he said. 'That's a good job he's got there.'

'How would you know? All you talked about was stupid cars.'

'Well, if you carry on like that you certainly won't keep him interested.'

'I don't know if I want to, after tonight.' She was almost shouting and her dad looked at her in amazement. He went back into the living room to watch the last minutes of the ten o'clock news.

Marie snatched the gloves and ran upstairs to her bedroom. She threw the gloves onto her dressing table, sat on the end of her bed and looked at herself in the mirror. Bill didn't care that they hadn't had a goodnight kiss, she knew that, he didn't care that they hadn't exchanged ten words all evening. He didn't even care that he'd shouted at her as he was leaving. And yet, she knew, with a sick feeling of certainty that he would ask her to marry him.

She picked up the gloves and slapped them together. She threw one into the air. Then she threw the other. She picked them up and started again. Clumsily, she began to juggle the gloves. She walked into the bathroom, juggling. She watched herself in the cabinet mirror until a glove fell into the basin. A dark stain appeared on the thumb from the dripping tap. She watched it for a while then dropped the other glove into the basin. Dark stains spread across the thick tan leather of the gloves. She picked up both gloves and tossed them into the toilet bowl. She pulled the chain. The gloves swirled and spun in the water. She pulled the chain again. One glove disappeared.

She walked out onto the landing then she crept down the stairs, carefully opened the front door and slid out of the house. She moved quickly down the garden path, through the gate and set off for the Prince of Orange.

THE BIRTHDAY CAKE

Marie always acted as if Mick was hers even after she got together with Bill. Of course, she did know him for longer. They stayed in touch for years, she said. But Deirdre was the one who went out with him.

Chelmsford's hero he was. Well, to the mods anyway. He was a scooter boy, hanging round town in his parka and his bluebeat hat, fiddling with his Lambretta outside the mod coffee bars of

Chelmsford, driving down to Clacton and Southend on Bank Holidays, getting into bundles with whoever was up for it, strutting his stuff, charming the girls.   Then one evening, it was dusk, about seven o'clock, Mick was in his parka with a fox tail flying behind on the aerial of his scooter, driving up and down in front of the bus station. A rocker came along on his big chugging bike, coming towards him in the middle of the road. Rockers didn't usually come that far up into town, they stayed by their coffee bar, the Long Bar, down by the Odeon. Perhaps he was new in town, perhaps he was lost, but perhaps he was looking for trouble. They drove towards each other, Mick and the rocker, in the middle of the road. Neither of them chickened out, which the mods said was at least something. They crashed. Mick lost his sight and the other guy lost an inch out of his leg.

Marie and Deirdre weren't there that night. They were up at the Moulsham Youth Club.

There was blood everywhere and someone scratched a message on the wall of the Co-op, Mick Crashed Here, but they painted over it. He was in hospital in London for months, having metal plates put in his head, his jaw rewired. He hadn't been wearing a crash helmet – nobody did in those days. They said he was lucky to be alive. He didn't think that. After they'd done everything they could at the hospital he went to Torquay to train to be blind. But it didn't work. He wouldn't be blind. He refused to be blind, even though he was blind. Wouldn't have a stick, wouldn't have a dog.

It was when he came back from Torquay, after Easter some time, that Marie and Deirdre met him. Marie was the first one to speak to him, in her dinner hour one day, in the Orpheus, the cellar coffee bar in London Road. He was with his friend Jeff. Someone introduced them. Everyone wanted to know Marie, she was so pretty.

They bumped into Mick once or twice on Saturdays, when he was in town with Jeff or some of his other mates. He looked quite cool in his long suede coat and his dark glasses. Jeff would nudge Mick and Mick would shout 'Watcha Marie! You're looking lovely today,' which she was but he didn't know. They never stopped to talk, he was three months younger than Marie. It mattered. She didn't introduce Deirdre. He didn't even know she was there.

Deirdre had just started work in Boots the chemist and she and Marie met every day at dinner time.

That Thursday Deirdre was taking her lunch break early. But she still went to the Orpheus. As she walked over to the counter the thin high guitar notes of 'Hi-Heel Sneakers' filled the cellar. This was a mod classic. Usually people would dance round the Orpheus in their suede Hush Puppies to this, Blond Don and Tap, mouthing the words, doing the moves, but today the place was almost empty. She tapped her foot in time to the music, and was ordering a drink when Mick came down the stairs with Jeff. They disappeared into one of the alcoves and then Jeff appeared behind her at the counter. 'Two coffees, please. I'll get that,' he said, as the manager put a glass of milk in front of Deirdre. 'You all on your own? Where's your mate?'

'Marie? She's at work.'

'Why aren't you at work then?'

'I could ask you the same thing.'

'Oh.' He laughed. 'You still at school then?'

'No!' she said, hotly. Still at school! 'I work in Boots.'

'Well, we'll know where to come when we need anything … important,' he said and laughed.

'What's your name again?'

'Deirdre.'

'Well, Deirdre –'

'Where's the fucking coffee?' Mick called from behind a pillar.

'It's coming!' Jeff shouted back.

'So's Christmas!'

'Thanks for the milk.' Deirdre turned away.

'That's all right,' Jeff said. 'Mick's paying.'

She went back to her seat.

The next Saturday she and Marie bumped into Mick and Jeff in Tindal Street, coming out of the men's clothes shop that was trying to be a boutique. Jeff nudged Mick and murmured to him. Mick said, 'All right Marie?' and she said, carelessly 'Yeah, all right, Mick?'

'We've been stocking up on the latest gear.'

'Oh,' said Marie. She wasn't interested.

'I just bought a couple of those button-down shirts,' Mick said. 'They'll all want to dance with me now.'

Jeff said, 'How's Boots, Deirdre?'

Mick said, 'Who the fuck's Deirdre?' and Marie laughed. 'That's what everyone says.'

'Hey girls,' Mick said, 'what you doing next Saturday morning? Can you come and pick me up? Jeff here won't be around.'

'I've got a job on the boats,' Jeff said.

He would be away for months, he said. And he was, through all the trouble. Deirdre's trouble. But that's how they started going up to Mick's house on the Army and Navy Roundabout on a Saturday morning. They'd ring the bell, and Mick would come to the door ready to go out. Mick would link arms with one or other of them and they would parade round the town, him in his bottle-green suede and his dark glasses and the girls in their straight skirts and Cleopatra hairdos.

In the evening, they would see him at the Corn Exchange, when the good groups came, the Who, the Yardbirds, Georgie Fame. Mick would be with his mates, Jeff, Blond Don, Tap, but there were always girls there, usually girls from out of town, girls Marie and Deirdre didn't know. He'd have his arm round one of them. Marie would see Deirdre gazing across the room and say, 'All right, let's go and talk to Mick.'

Over they'd go and 'Hallo darlings,' he'd say. Sometimes he was drunk and he'd stumble against

Marie and put his arm round her, and the other girl would slip away, Somehow Marie always managed to get rid of the other girl. Sometimes they'd all go up to the Golden Fleece and Mick would buy them a drink. Marie drank gin and bitter lemon, Deirdre chose rum and blackcurrant although she didn't really like it. Once or twice Deirdre asked him to dance. Mick would only dance to slow dances. 'I'm not making an arse of myself trying to dance fast,' he said. Marie wouldn't dance with him. 'He might get ideas,' she said.

One night Mick and Deirdre swayed slowly to Graham Bond singing 'St James Infirmary'. He was humming softly in her ear. She could smell the beer on his breath. She tried to make conversation, though he wasn't really interested. He didn't care about work, he didn't care about the people who came in to the chemist's.

'How do you get your hair so lovely and shiny,' he said, running his hand over her head.

'I put vinegar on it.'

'You what?' he said. He was laughing.

'It makes it silky,' she said. She shook her head under his nose and his lips brushed her cheek. She turned her head and then he was kissing her, breathing hard. His mouth tasted sour, the alcohol strong on his tongue. He was almost 18 and she was 16.

They went out for two months and three weeks. Deirdre loved it. She and Marie still called at his house together, except for that once, that one time. But now when they walked arm in arm it was because he was hers.

And it was her job to tell him what the mods were wearing, so he could keep up with the fashion, describing what people looked like. She said, 'Does it matter that you don't know what I look like?' And he said, 'I know what you look like, a bottle of Sarson's vinegar.'

And now, at the Corn Exchange there were no other girls, just her. He put his arm round her.

He was always loud and a bit coarse, when they were out, swearing at people and ready for a fight. Often she had to pull his arm and plead, 'Mick, don't!' But when he brought her home he made the taxi park half way down the road, by the farm houses and he held her tight, whispering in her ear, stroking her face, learning her features.

It was all going so well. She made him a cake for his eighteenth birthday, three eggs, her mum went mad, eggs were expensive. Icing, mock cream, candles. It looked almost professional. She took it round to his nan's house, on her own. Marie had gone up to London for the day with her new bloke Bill. Otherwise Deirdre wouldn't have dared.

His nan was out. They were alone. It just happened. But she did love him. She thought they'd get married.

About a week later her dad lost his job and she and her mum were shunted off to her nan's in Lincoln. Mick didn't write but then she didn't expect him to. He hated typing and he hated the fact that if he wrote with a pen his handwriting looked like a child's. And they didn't have a phone.

The night Deirdre decided to tell her mum, she was about three months gone, feeling sick, sitting in the kitchen, waiting for her nan to go into the living room to watch Coronation Street. They cried, they argued, all soft sobs and hissing, so her nan didn't hear. Her mum asked if Mick knew.

Deirdre looked at her mum - of course Mick didn't know, Mick probably thought because she worked at Boots it was all under control. Deirdre laughed at the thought, and her mum slapped her face. Then her hand flew to her mouth. 'I'm sorry,' she whispered. She wiped her hand on her apron. 'Do you want to tell him?'

Deirdre shook her head, what was the point? Marie had written saying she'd seen him with a girl from Braintree. 'He forgot you soon enough,' she wrote. 'He even pretended not to hear me when I said hello.'

'Have you told Marie?' her mum asked.

Deirdre hadn't told her. She knew Marie would react badly – be too nice to her, or tell Mick. Or not tell Mick.

'Right,' her mum took a deep breath. 'You don't say a word to anyone. It'll be my baby. You'll be the big sister. You can go out and get a job and maybe not waste all of your life. I'll deal with your nan and your dad. They can't say anything.' Deirdre's mum had had to get married when she fell pregnant with Deirdre. She hadn't been allowed to wear a white dress.

Deirdre's mum thought it was all Marie's fault – with her pretty face and the fact she'd left school first. 'Only a term earlier,' Deirdre said. Her mum said Marie should have stopped Deirdre going anywhere near Mick. And Deirdre thought it was

Marie's fault, she shouldn't have gone out with Bill that day, and she should certainly have stopped Mick seeing other people after they left. She should have known Deirdre needed him, whether or not she was having a baby.

By the time they moved back to Chelmsford the baby was ten months old and Mick had gone to live in London. He'd got some job book-keeping or something. So much for not liking typing. Marie was courting strong with Bill. Deirdre was her bridesmaid when they got married. They didn't see much of each other afterwards. It was hard when they did meet, because Deirdre wanted to tell her about the baby, Catherine, explain that she wasn't her sister, it was her daughter. But she couldn't, she hadn't told Catherine yet, and anyway Marie was into casseroles and curtains and she had her own children.

Catherine was growing up. She was lovely, glowing skin, big brown eyes. Put her in a bottle-green suede, Deirdre thought, with a pair of dark glasses, and you'd think Mick had walked into the room.

Sometimes, if Marie dropped round to leave a Christmas card, or a birthday present, she'd talk to

Catherine, look at her for a long while. But if she saw any resemblance, she never said.

THE GIFT

There was a boy called Ronnie Dee. He was older than me, 18 maybe 19. He had a smooth face, dark eyes, short dark hair in the mod way, and a navy blue leather. He was quiet, but he told little jokes and then he would turn and smile at me. When he came down the Orpheus, the mods' coffee bar, someone would put "King Bee" by the Rolling Stones on the juke box. Bee, Dee. Blond Don would start to sing, 'I'm a King Dee.' He'd shout, 'Turn it off!' but I don't think he really minded.

He had a girl-friend, Christine Lindon, from round our way. They were supposed to be courting strong, but she didn't come down the Orpheus very much, a couple of times. I only ever spoke to her once. I knew her from primary school, she was in the year above me. I didn't think she was very pretty so I had as good a chance as anyone.

Sandra and I sat at the table by the foot of the stairs which was the only way in to the Orpheus. It was right by the juke box. I would make smart remarks to him when he came over.

He'd say, 'What d'you want, girls?' I'd say, 'Mary Wells.' She had a big hit. I'd say, 'I want to hear "Little Boy",' which was the B side. And he'd start to sing 'Nothing you can do can make me untrue.' Which was "My Guy", the A side. And I'd say, 'No.' He'd make a stupid face and say, 'Silly me.' Then he'd put on the Supremes after all.

This particular day, Sandra and I had a row. It was a Saturday afternoon, we were on the bus into town. It was a real row. Usually, we'd make something up, so that we could flounce off and be in two places at once, and find out what twice as many people were doing. But this time it was real. It was because we were going to see Wilson Pickett that night and I had to be in at 11 o'clock.

'Why won't your mum let you stay out just a little bit later?' she said, 'Saturday's not a school day.'

'She thinks drastic things happen late at night.'

'How does she know? She hasn't been out since people grew their own Shredded Wheat.'

'She says she can't make exceptions for special occasions because I have too many. She wants me to come home in one piece.'

'Yeah, as if anyone's going to look at you.'

'Thanks.'

'Wilson Picket's biggest hit is "The Midnight Hour." How sensible are we going to look leaving at quarter past ten to catch the bus? We always look like idiots.' She paused. 'It might help if we didn't have to catch the bus.'

'It's not my fault I can't afford taxis. You go to work and earn money!' I was shouting.

'You're just … just too young!' she said, and got off the bus at the railway station, even though we'd paid to go to the Regent.

When I got off I waited to see if she'd come and meet me, but she didn't, so I cut through the ground floor of the Co-op and out on to London Road.

It was the Whitsun bank holiday and it was sunny, so there weren't very many people in the Orpheus, most of them had gone down to Southend or Clacton. There were just some young kids from the Westlands Estate, wearing parkas and talking too loudly and Mr Flaxman, the manager, behind the counter. After about half an hour, Ronnie came down the stairs. 'Watcha,' he said, glancing round the room. He went up to the counter and said something to Flaxman who shrugged in reply.

Ronnie looked over at me. 'Have you seen Tap and those?' I shook my head. Tap worked in the boutique. He was a big mod.

'I haven't seen him.'

'Well, if anyone would know it would be you. Don't you two ever go home?' he said. 'Where is your mate anyway?'

'She's probably gone off somewhere with Tap,' I said.

Ronnie ordered a coffee, then turned back to me. 'Do you want something?'

He said it so casually, so naturally, as if this was what we always did, chatted, he bought the drinks, we sat together. I was so thrilled, I said, 'No thanks.'

He turned away.

I'd spoiled everything. What would Sandra do? I went across to him and said, 'I've changed my mind. Can I have a glass of milk?' He laughed. 'I'll bring it over,' he said.

I went back to the table and pushed my still hot cup of coffee away, as if it had never belonged to me.

He brought the milk to the table, and stood flipping through the juke box. 'Where Did Our Love Go?' he said.

'Route 66,' I replied.

'You Really Got Me. How Do You Do It?'

'Hi-Heel Sneakers.'

'Have you got a threepenny bit?'

'I don't know that one, but I think Cilla Black wants to make a cover version.' I was looking in my purse. 'I haven't got any change.'

'I'll ask Flaxman,' he said, walking to the counter.

One of the young boys in a parka came across and put 6d in the juke box. He selected one record then stood flipping the pages round. The first notes of "King Bee" filled the alcove. Ronnie came back. 'You taking the piss?' he said to the boy.

'Sorry mate, didn't know this one was banned.'

'Fuck off,' Ronnie said. 'You're not from round here are you?'

'I've got as much right to be here as you have.'

'Why don't you fuck off to Clacton? You can cause as much trouble as you like down there.'

'Yeah, well, why aren't you there?' the boy said defiantly.

'Some of us have to work. And when you're old enough to drive a car, you'll know they're a lot more expensive than tin-can scooters. And girls don't come cheap these days.'

He smiled at me. I didn't know what to think.

I heard the door at the top of the stairs swing open and Tap, the big mod, appeared. He lifted his head towards Ronnie. 'We're just going shopping,' he said.

'I'll come with you.' Ronnie turned to me. 'I'll get you something. What do you fancy?'

I smiled, I knew this time I really should say nothing, thank you, no, no. Shopping was Chelmsford mods' word for shoplifting. But the offer was so tempting.

He put his finger under my chin and kissed me. It was a soft, sweet kiss, the first proper kiss I'd ever had. 'See you later,' he said and ran up the stairs, two at a time.

There was a draught of air and Sandra clattered down into the room, but she wasn't on her own. She was with Jacky. Jacky was a mod but she was a bit too flash. She had a black and white dogtooth coat with a leather collar and a crochet dress. She worked in an office in London, and sometimes in the evenings she helped Flaxman out behind the counter. So she could afford the clothes. Jacky didn't speak to us usually. I thought we'd agreed she was common, wearing too much make-up, shouting across the room. She had a thick husky voice and a London accent, and she swore and smoked. She thought she was the big It, and people said she'd Done It with more than one boy. But later Sandra said that was all talk and she was just someone who knew how to talk to boys, she was a boys' girl.

She and Sandra bought glasses of Coke and lemon and came and sat with me under the stairs. 'Since when did you start drinking milk?' Sandra said.

'Since just now,' I said.

They were talking about Ready Steady Go, the

mods' TV programme, which everyone watched on Fridays. Jacky said, 'All right, who would you be and what would you sing in the mime competition?' I chose Dusty Springfield, singing 'You don't have to say you love me' but Sandra and Jacky laughed at me, because I didn't look at all like her, I didn't backcomb my hair, and, Jacky said slyly, 'no mod girl would ever wear that much eye make-up.' I wanted to say to her, 'You do,' but I thought she'd have a go at me, and I didn't know if Sandra would be on my side.

Then Ronnie and Tap came back, talking loudly and laughing down the stairs. Ronnie nodded a greeting at us. Sandra nudged me in surprise, she didn't know he'd been talking to me, and I wasn't going to say anything, not with Jacky sitting there with her big mouth. But Jacky called out, 'Hello boys. Get home all right last night? Ooh, I love your car, Ronnie.'

He and Tap went over to the counter.

Jacky gazed at them, then turned to me and Sandra. 'There's one who doesn't care if you wear a lot of eye make-up, as long as you don't wear much else! Know what I mean?'

'No,' I said.

'Linda!' Sandra said, meaning don't be so stupid.

But I didn't want to know. He wasn't like that, that wasn't him. He had a girlfriend, even if I didn't like her.

'Mmm, yeah,' said Jacky. 'And when he runs his hands up and down your back. Oooh.' She shuddered.

I wanted to kill her. I wanted to kill him.

We were putting on our coats, going home for our tea when Ronnie stuck his head round the corner. 'Here,' he said, 'I got this for you.' We all stared at him. It was a small bottle of 4711 Eau-de-Cologne on a gold and turquoise card. He gave it to me. It was a present for me. Sandra looked surprised.

'Oh, watcha Jacky,' he said, 'didn't see you there. All right?'

'Much better now,' Jacky said and laughed her husky, dirty laugh. 'So what did you get for me?'

'There wasn't a shop fancy enough to find the right thing for you,' he said to her, and went back to talk to Tap.

'And you got Eau-de-Cologne,' she snorted.

At least I got something, I wanted to say, but I felt stupid. When we went home for tea I left the bottle of Eau-de-Cologne on the seat.

Ronnie didn't come down the Orpheus much after that. Perhaps he came down once more, with Christine. I know there was one time I talked to her. He was probably in the toilet. She came over to the juke box, pretended to be looking for something to put on. 'Have you got a threepenny bit?' she asked me. 'You're down here a lot,' she said, as I rummaged in my purse, trying to look natural. 'Is there anyone else he talks to?'

'Not me!' I said.

'I didn't mean you!' She looked as if that was the most idiotic idea in the world. 'No, what about her?' She looked over at the counter, where Jacky was laughing with some boys who'd just come in from Mile End.

'Jacky?' I said.

He didn't come any more. Someone said there were problems with Christine, it was on, it was off. I hoped it was off.

And then one night a rocker came running down the stairs, in his greasy leather jacket, and thick boots, and shouted 'Who knows Ronnie Dee?'

There'd been an accident. Ronnie was driving along the A12, he overtook the biker, and then he went under a bridge and smashed into one of the pillars.

Someone whispered that it might have been suicide. I couldn't believe that. He smiled so much. But I wondered whether if I'd accepted the Eau-de-Cologne, it would have been different. I could have worn it and we could have talked about how nice it smelt. I'd have made up for Christine leaving him. Well it would have sort of been my duty, really. I'd done the right thing, told her about Jacky, she deserved to know, but I had to stay around and pick up the pieces.

Sandra and I were in the Orpheus, sitting under the stairs, when Tap came down, after the funeral, in his moddy mohair suit, and thin tie. Jacky was helping behind the counter. 'All right Tap?' she said.

'Fuck off, Jacky,' Tap said. 'You've caused enough trouble.'

'What did I say?' She came over to us and wiped our table with a grey rag. 'Shame, isn't it? He was such a nice bloke, Ronnie,' She sighed. 'You know what I wish? I wish I could have kissed him, just once.'

'You should have done it when you were having

sex,' I said.

'You what?' she said. 'Me and Ronnie? You're joking. Chance would have been a fine thing. Now Tap. Whole other kettle of fish, if you get my meaning.'

THE WALKING HOLIDAY

The Brady family were Catholic. Our family were Congregationalists, but I knew Sandra's church, because when we were young I'd sit in the pews while she went to confession, and after we would buy a tuppenny bag of stale cakes from the baker's in Moulsham Street and sit and eat them in the park.

And we still walked that way now, towards the church in London Road, but before we got that far, we passed the Orpheus, the mods' coffee bar, and we had to go in there. Sandra said it was a kind of religion, being a mod, and going to the Orpheus was like going to church. We had to go almost every day, and then on Saturdays we went to the Corn Exchange, the mods' Cathedral, to see visiting priests, Georgie Fame and Zoot Money.

But going to the Corn Exchange was only the start. Coming home on the eleven o'clock bus we made plans. She'd pass her driving test, get a car and we'd travel, far away, a kind of pilgrimage, to Devon and Cornwall, get jobs in a hotel, live there and have adventures.

The furthest I was allowed to go with Sandra that summer was to the Isle of Wight for a walking holiday. We had no intention of walking anywhere but the holiday was organised by an institution which people in my mum's church knew about and so my mum and dad said it was all right for us to go on our own.

Marie said that she and Bill would drive us down to Southampton in the Mini. They were engaged at that point. We would rather have gone on the train, that was going to be part of the adventure and also Bill was sarcastic, but Sandra's mum said she was ungrateful.

When we got in the car Bill said Sandra and I had to pay for the petrol, Super, there and back. 'I've got to get home. I'm not staying in Southampton for a week waiting to bring you back, am I?' he sneered. 'And I have to pay for wear and tear.' So it was actually more expensive.

'At least we're going half way in a Mini,' Sandra said. 'Starting as we mean to go on.'

It was a hot day and we sat sweating and nauseated in the back of the car. At Basingstoke Sandra started singing Que Sera Sera, which was a joke because she and I had always sung that when we were little.

'You're only going to the Isle of Wight,' Bill said, 'Not Paris. Anyway you don't even know what you're singing about.'

'Linda can speak French,' Sandra said.

'All right Miss Brainbox, say something in French then.'

Sandra and I rolled our eyes at each other.

'Quelle est cette langueur qui pénètre mon coeur?' I said.

'Yeah, and what does that mean?'

It was a poem we'd learned at school but I

couldn't remember what it was about.

Bill laughed. 'You sure you can speak French? Didn't even sound French,' He flared his nostrils.

'You can't even speak English,' Sandra said.

'Oh yeah?' said Bill. 'I can speak more French than her. Voulez-vous coucher avec moi ce soir?'

'No thank you,' I said, looking out of the window.

We were stuck in a traffic jam and Bill got out to stretch his legs. Then the queue started to move and everyone behind was hooting and Bill had to jump back in. Marie shouted at Bill and he told her to stop shouting and she shouted 'I'm not shouting!' and he bellowed 'Yes, you fucking are,' and then she threw something at him. He slammed on the brakes and the car behind bashed into us. We had to pull off the road and swap names and addresses. And then we spent an hour trying to find her engagement ring. So we missed our ferry.

When we finally did trail off the boat in Cowes there were no taxis left. We gazed hopelessly along the deserted streets. 'Don't say we've got to walk,' Sandra said.

We looked at each other.

We walked a few yards in the direction of the setting sun, because we knew we needed to go west. 'Don't they have bus stops in the country?' Sandra asked. She stopped to shake a stone from her slingback, grabbing my arm for balance. 'I told you it was stupid coming on a walking holiday.'

'At least you've worn your shoes before today,' I said.

Sandra stuck out her thumb and in two minutes an old Morris Traveller with wood on the sides pulled up. A little old man and a little old woman looked at us enquiringly.

'We're going to Freshwater Bay,' Sandra said.

'If you'd like a lift and you don't mind dogs, please do get in,' said the woman.

Sandra smiled at me triumphantly.

On our first morning at the House, we picked up our packed lunch and got on the coach with everyone else and went to Shanklin. There were some girls about our age in the group, sitting at the front of the coach with proper boots on. Everyone else was just old, with glowing cheeks and wrinkles.

In Shanklin the walkers strode away towards the hills, adjusting their knapsacks, moving their arms stiffly in their anoraks and thick jumpers, while Sandra and I, wearing our pinstriped skirts and suede jackets, slithered off to Woolworths. We found the nearest railings and leaned against them, waiting.

We were looking for any sort of scooter, even a Lambretta 125. A Mini was of course our dream but glancing round it didn't seem likely. Everyone was about 112 and from their clothes you'd say they were all on walking holidays.

Sandra was worried about the effect her hair might have on our chances. The colour was Copper Dream. I'd done it for her, but not very well and it was a bit intense at the back.

'You'll be all right as long as you face people,' I said. I liked it, but what did I know? I was having trouble with my own hair. I'd grown out my fringe and I'd pulled it back into a ponytail, then clipped it under like a bun, but I wasn't sure about it.

'Do you think we should have come on this holiday?' Sandra said, squinting at the sky. 'They're all a bit posh.'

'Are they?'

'You know they are.'

We waited for an hour.

And then a pale blue Mini drew up. The one

climbing out of the passenger seat wore braces with his jeans. The driver wore a fair-isle jumper. They stood beside the car and looked around.

Sandra went across to them and asked them where Ventnor was. They laughed. By the time she came back she'd found out they were from Catford and they'd caught the same ferry that we had. Plus they'd never been to Chelmsford.

They drove away and we wandered through the streets until we found a park. We sat on the grass, and spread out our packed lunch, cheese and Pan-Yan sandwiches, Wagon Wheels, an apple and a pear.

'We'd have been better off staying in Chelmsford,' said Sandra on the third day. We were lying on our beds and we'd just had an argument about toothpaste. 'There'd be people to talk to and we wouldn't have to eat hard pears. And also, we wouldn't have to sit with those posh girls every meal time.'

'Janet and Marilyn? They're all right.'

'That's because you're used to girls like that. At your school everyone's fresh air and jolly hockey sticks.'

'Not all of them.'

'I don't know what they're talking about half the time. And they laugh at us, they laugh at you and me.'

'They don't.'

'They do. They think we're two girls from Essex, who don't like walking. And your voice changes when you talk to them.'

'It doesn't.'

That evening, after we'd been to a lecture on flower arranging, the 'young people'- anyone who was under 30 and over twelve - met in the kitchen. Janet and Marilyn, Sandra and I and a couple of other girls sat on benches round the big wooden table. I had decided to have cocoa for a change, and Sandra was the only one having coffee. As she slung her coffee spoon in the sink she said, 'All right, where was everyone on the night that President Kennedy was shot?'

I cringed. They'd think we were really stupid.

I knew where I'd been , because I kept a diary. I'd been coming out of guides. Sandra had come to meet me and told me. But why would anyone else remember? But they did. They all said something.

One girl said her nanny had told her when she and her sister were having their bath, and another said someone in her dormitory, called Angela, had been rung up specially by her mother and she had cried, and then the whole dormitory had cried.

They asked Sandra where she'd been. She looked at me, then said, 'At home. On our estate.'

The next day was a free day for everyone. 'Where are they all going?' said Sandra, peering through the windows of the breakfast room. Small groups were forming in front of the house. 'They're going for another walk and they don't even have to!'

Sandra and I washed our hair, and Sandra wrote a postcard to Danny, her boyfriend, who was back inside for shoplifting two necklaces, worth £1 17s 6d each, from Bonds, the biggest department store in Chelmsford. He'd been in breach of his suspended sentence.

In the afternoon we wandered into the centre of the village and found a café called 'Jen's Coffee Bar'. It had a faded orange and white striped awning and there was a blackboard in the window with the words 'fish and chips' chalked in capitals.

'The state of this!' Sandra said, as we walked up

to the counter.

'Well, it's almost like the Orpheus,' I said, wanting Sandra to enjoy it.

'Apart from the fact that this is above ground, all the lights are on, and everyone in here's over 60. Yeah, it's just like the Orpheus. Two glasses of milk please.'

'At least they've got a juke box.'

'Yeah, with Mantovani on, or Joe Loss, I bet. There's not a single mod in here.'

I looked round the room. 'Perhaps it's a rocker bar. There's someone over there wearing American tan stockings.'

'I think those are support-hose, Linda. Why is everyone so old on the Isle of Wight?'

'Well at least they're out and about.'

'Yeah, out the house, up the doctor's, down to the chemists, and into Casualty.' We laughed. 'Oh no,' Sandra groaned. 'Look who's here.' The posh girls were walking in. They smiled at us and sat on the other side of the room.

I stood over the jukebox, scouring the list of records. I put in threepence and after a few seconds the eery organ notes and the yearning voice of Alan Price singing 'I'll Put a Spell on you' filled the room. I thought about Chelmsford, the mods I was missing, the chat, the jokes. I looked at Sandra, she was staring at her drink. She must have been feeling the same.

I looked over at Janet and Marilyn to see if they'd caught the mood. But they were chatting quietly, not even listening to the music, and then they drained their orange squash and left, without staying to the end of the record.

'They're boarding-school girls, that's why they don't get it,' Sandra said. 'They like walking. What do you expect?'

The next morning at breakfast, Janet and Marilyn brought their trays to our table just as we were piling up our dishes.

'Ooh, porridge,' Sandra whispered.

'Are you enjoying the holiday?' said Janet.

Sandra groaned.

'Yeah, it's … good,' I said.

'Not what you're used to, perhaps.'

'We walk in Chelmsford,' Sandra said. 'I walk to work and she walks to school.'

There was a pause. Janet and Marilyn began talking about A levels.

'And we walk on the Ban the Bomb march, don't we Lin?'

'Yes,' I said. 'The Campaign for Nuclear Disarmament.'

'Is that the badge you wear on your coat?' Janet said.

They'd noticed! But they didn't know what it was. 'And I play netball for my house.'

Sandra threw me a glance and I expected her to say, 'Only for the second team, and only because they're desperate,' but she didn't. There was silence.

'Our school's got a good all-round reputation,' I said. 'Apparently.'

'Oh yes?' Janet said. 'What school is that?'

'Chelmsford High School,' Sandra said.

'You're at Cheltenham?'

'Chelmsford,' Sandra said.

'Of course.

'So you've left school now?' Janet said politely, turning to Sandra.

'I have,' Sandra said. 'I work at Marconi's. You know, so everyone can listen to Pick of the Pops on the radio.' Sandra looked at me. 'We've got postcards to write.'

We carried our trays over to the kitchen hatch.

It was the last night. We were in the House, packing our cases, with Sandra trying to catch a moth before it got into our clothes and ate them all on the way home, when there was a knock on the door.

Sandra was standing on the bed shouting at the moth and I was cowering in the corner of the room laughing. We both fell silent.

Janet's head appeared round the door. She looked at us and almost shrugged. She said, 'There are some people to see you, downstairs.'

Sandra and I looked at each other, thrilled and appalled. We knew who it was.

We ran along the corridor, arguing who had given away our address, and peered over the banister.

It was the boys from Catford, standing in the large lobby, looking out of place, trying not to care.

'I don't like yours,' we murmured in unison as we got to the bottom of the stairs.

Their names were Carl and Mark. 'Like Karl Marx,' I said, as we walked over to the Mini.

'Very funny,' said Carl, the driver.

'I expect people say that a lot,' I said.

'No.' He opened the passenger door. 'What's

that badge, then? Ban-the-Bomb? You into all that free love?'

'No.'

We suggested going to the coffee bar. Sandra and I sat silently in the back of the car, as if the people from the House would be able to hear any conversation we might have. 'There's a juke box,' I said apologetically as we pulled up outside.

'We're just about to close,' said the woman behind the counter.

'Well, can't we buy something and take it away?' Mark said.

'We can have a picnic,' I said.

'At 7 o'clock at night?' said Sandra. 'There's a pub near the place we're staying in.'

'There's a pub near us,' said Carl.

'But that's the other side of the island,' I said.

'We'll bring you back.'

'We'd better go to the pub near us,' Sandra said. 'There'll be more drinking time.'

As we drove to the pub, she sat in the back with Mark.

We stopped at a pub called the Royal Oak.

'This isn't the one,' I said. 'This is miles from where we're staying.'

'They have good beer,' Carl said. I looked round at Sandra. She rolled her eyes at me. I got out of the car. Sandra and Mark climbed out of the back seats.

Sandra looked at her watch. 'We haven't got time, now, actually. She has to be in bed with a cup of Horlicks by half past nine.' I opened my mouth. 'It's all right,' she said, 'we'll make our own way from here.'

I gazed at her in silence.

As we turned the first bend in the road I said, 'What was wrong with him?'

'He was trying to get into my knickers, that's what was wrong with him. And they weren't even my best knickers.' Sandra looked round. 'Where are we?' We walked along the lane towards a signpost. 'Freshwater Bay, seven miles,' she read. 'All right, Lin?'

'Yeah.'

'Just think of this as the walking part of our walking holiday,' Sandra said, and linked her arm through mine.

MARIE'S WEDDING

Marie was getting married.   She was going to wear a long, semi-fitted dress in plain white satin, have two bridesmaids, and a reception for fifty in the new community centre on our estate.   Deirdre and Marie's sister Sandra were the bridesmaids.   Their dresses were empire line, made of pink and white net, with puff sleeves. I had hoped Marie would ask me to be a bridesmaid, but it was a long time since we'd been real friends.

The wedding would be held in the Church of the

Immaculate Conception because the Brady family were Catholic. Our family were Congregationalists, but I knew their church because over the years I had occasionally gone to confession with Marie and Sandra, sitting in the dark incense filled church as they said Hail Marys to the priest.

And now Marie was going there to marry Bill, long, tall, sarcastic Bill. He had the mini, he had the sheepskin coat. But there was still something cold about him. And Sandra and I knew that Marie didn't really love him.

Marie loved Johnny Brown. Johnny lived in the flats over the shops. In fact, it was Sandra and I who met him first.

He had an old green van that he parked in the bay in front of the shops and he was always outside, with the bonnet up, checking this, tapping that. On the evenings we went to buy a four-penny bag of chips, we started saying hello. Then we stopped for a chat. One day Sandra gave him a set of spanners that her dad was throwing out. Sandra really fancied him. 'I've got a plan,' she said to me.

One evening Johnny drove past when Sandra and Marie were walking up Sperry Drive, on the way home from work. He gave them a lift. They were all squashed into the front seat.

Sandra said to me, 'See? The plan's working.' But the next thing that happened was he started going out with Marie.

They didn't really go out. He never had much money. Working in a shop didn't pay that well. They went for drives and he made her laugh. Sometimes we went too, sitting on cushions in the back of his van that smelt of oil and petrol. We went to Colchester castle, or Maldon to look at the boats. And he'd tell awful jokes. 'Why is an elephant grey?' 'Dunno.' 'So you can tell it from a raspberry which is red!' 'Why does an elephant paint its nails red?' '?' 'So it can hide in a cherry tree.' He said they were greengrocer's jokes, because of the fruit.

Sometimes I would sit in the bedroom while Sandra did Marie's hair. I held the clips. I would say, 'How's Johnny?' to make conversation.

Sandra always said, 'She lo-o-o-ves him. She wants to marry him.'

Marie would look at us both in the mirror and say, 'Shut up. You're just kids.' She almost spoke to herself. 'You've got to get married. There's no point if you don't get married.' If I dropped a clip and had to hunt for it in the pattern on the rug, she said, 'Watch out Linda, if you end up wearing glasses, you won't get married. No-one will want you.'

But her mum and dad didn't like Johnny. He'd only been to the Secondary Mod and he was a loser. He didn't have a proper job, working in the greengrocer's. And a greengrocer's on our estate, not even in town. Mrs Brady worked in the grocer's. They wanted something better for their daughter.

Marie met Bill at the Youth Club. He'd been to the Grammar School. Sandra said Bill liked Marie because she was pretty. He said she looked good in the Mini. But it was on and off. One night when Sandra and I were playing records in their living room they had an argument and Bill called Marie a slag for two-timing him with Johnny. Then they got engaged.

On the morning of the wedding I went over to Sandra's house to help. Trixie, the hairdresser who lived next door, came round to do everyone's hair. The bride and bridesmaids were all having it pulled back from their faces and clipped into curls then dotted with flowers. It was a look I'd dreamed of achieving, but my hair wasn't long enough. And I wasn't a bridesmaid. After she'd done everyone else's hair, Trixie brushed through mine and did a lot of back-combing which I really didn't like, but I didn't know how to stop her because Mrs Brady was paying.

'Like your beehive,' Sandra said.

Then we all went upstairs for the bride and bridesmaids to put on their dresses. While Marie slid into her dress in the bedroom, Sandra, Deirdre and I squeezed into the bathroom. Deirdre looked in the mirror and burst into tears. 'I'm a pink and white striped elephant with sausages on my head,' she said. 'No, you aren't,' Sandra and I said together, though I could see she had put on a bit of weight.

'I can't go out looking like this,' Deirdre said. Her eyes were getting all red. I wanted to step in and say, 'I'll do it! I'll be the bridesmaid,' and save the day. Deirdre could wear my smart olive green dress with the long sleeves, and I'd happily wear hers, but then Sandra's mum knocked on the door of the bathroom and told us to hurry up because she was bursting and she couldn't go to the outdoor lav in her new costume. Quickly, Sandra dabbed grey eyeliner on to Deirdre's puffy eyes, and white lip-shimmer on her lips, and we all went down to the front room, and Marie, Deirdre and Sandra posed, smiling, for the photographer to take the photos. The bride and bridesmaids.

A large black Rolls Royce had pulled up outside the house and Marie, Mr Brady and Sandra and Deirdre climbed in. My dad had cleaned our Vauxhall specially and he was driving behind, taking me and Mrs Brady and Deirdre's mum. We drove through the estate, past the neighbours at their gates, nodding, and smiling, past the shops, and past the community centre, where the reception was being held.

The wedding passed in a blur of 'Here comes the Bride' and a boring sermon. I cried although I wasn't sure why. I heard Sandra sniff too, as she stood behind Marie, shifting from foot to foot.

We drove back to the reception. I was seated with the relatives from Ipswich for the lunch. As we went to our places, Sandra whispered, 'At least you haven't got to sit next to the priest,' which she did.

Their cousin Freddy was there. I liked Freddy, even though he was a rocker. He was 18 and he always shared a car with me on the Dodgems when we went to the fair at Ipswich.

We all admired the serviettes with 'Bill and Marie' printed on them in curly silver script, and the relatives wondered who'd paid for that, and then we ate the chicken salad and trifle. I could see the priest leaning over to speak to Sandra and we rolled our eyes at each other and then he looked and I made a very serious and holy face. When we got to the toasts Bill made a sneery speech about the bridesmaids, and I looked into my glass and wouldn't laugh, then the cake was cut and the tables were moved to the back of the room.

The dancing began. Freddy was doing the records. His collection was a bit fifties, like his slicked back blond hair and his bootlace tie. Sandra went over and said she had a request from the bride, would he start with Brenda Lee please, but if he couldn't manage that, her own request was anything by the Four Tops, really please. Sandra and I couldn't do our dance to that old-fashioned, rocker music. We had practiced a special neat tight mod jive, a Wedding Jive, just for today, but you needed good music. Disappointingly, Freddy had a whole album of Brenda Lee, and Marie and Bill moved silently on to the dance floor and started waltzing.

Deirdre was sitting with her mum so Sandra had to dance with the Best Man, an old friend of Bill's who she quite liked. I flicked listlessly through Freddy's records.

'Hey, what about some beer for a working man?' he called to Mrs Brady. She looked confused and murmured something about Bill having said he'd take care of that side of things and she and Mr Brady exchanged a worried look.

Sandra beckoned me to go into the toilets with her. She had a rip under the arm of her dress. 'Marie's going to kill me,' she said.

'She won't know, will she?' I said. 'She'll be off on her honeymoon before you have to take it off.'

'She'll know,' she said.

I was trying to close the gap with a safety pin when Marie came in. We both looked up guiltily.

But Marie was crying. Her hair was coming down. Her heels were bleeding where her white satin shoes rubbed. Her mum had said something to Bill about the beer and now he was upset. It was all going wrong. She wished she hadn't got married.

I wanted to say 'Well, what did you expect? You chose the wrong one.' But I didn't.

Sandra carefully pinned back her curls and said it would all be OK.

I looked at Marie in the mirror and said, 'You look really nice.'

She snorted and said, 'Thanks.'

Freddy asked me to go over to the Off Licence with him, to help him get some beer. I was pleased he'd asked me. He was nice and tall and I liked his arms. He always pushed back his sleeves when he was choosing a record, and his arms were strong and sinewy. We crossed over to the row of shops that included the grocer's and the greengrocer's.

Some of the wedding guests had parked their cars in front of the shops. Outside the newsagents was an old van. 'The state of that and the price of fish,' Freddy said. 'Who'd come to a wedding in an old banger like that?'

I shrugged. The bonnet was down.

We walked into the Off Licence with its fluorescent lighting and faint smell of a pub at opening time. 'Good job you weren't a bridesmaid,' Freddy said. When he said the word 'bridesmaid' it had three syllables. 'You couldn't go lugging old crates of beer in one of those dresses.'

'You didn't say anything about lugging crates of beer,' I said.

'Why do you think I asked you to help me?' he said. He looked at my face. 'Only kidding!' He gave me a hug. There was no-one from the family here to see, so he could.

I tried to drag it out as long as possible, looking at the crisps and asking the price of Babycham, but Freddy wanted to get back. Although he'd put on a Bachelors' LP he said the Bachelors were really only good for two songs at a time. I said, 'As many as that?' He laughed.

The man in the Off Licence heaved a crate of Mackesons on to the counter and Freddy paid. A piece of confetti drifted through the air. The man said, 'Having a good day?' Freddy looked at me and grinned. He gave me another hug.

'Well, I hope you'll both be very happy,' the man said.

As we came out of the Off Licence there was a wolf whistle and a shout. I didn't look round. My heart started thumping.

Freddy shouted, 'Clear off, she's taken.'

I hoped he meant me. 'It's just Johnny,' I said.

'I know who it is,' he said.

84

Back in the hall I looked for Sandra. I wanted to tell her Johnny was outside. She could decide if Marie should know.

Freddy said, 'Open us a beer and you can pick a record.'

I chose 'Running Scared'. As Roy Orbison's voice sobbed through the room Freddy led me onto the dance floor. He swung me round then pulled me close. 'Don't mess this up for her,' he murmured.

'Who put this on?' Marie said, marching up to the turntable. 'Have I got to choose all the music? Freddy, we want to dance properly.' She chose Wake Up Little Susie and Freddy didn't protest. Marie moved towards Bill, beckoning him with her index finger. I turned to follow her. 'Stay here,' Freddy said. 'You can choose the next one.'

Sandra came over to the record table. Marie was going home to change into her Going Away outfit, she said. I looked at Freddy and he shook his head and put his finger to his lips.

'Home!' I said to her. 'How? Is the Rolls still here?'

'She's going to walk, stupid. It's only up the road.'

Only up the road meant walking past the shops,

walking past the van outside the newsagent's. I stared at Sandra. 'What - what about her feet?'

'They're all right now. Deirdre gave her some plasters.'

Perhaps the van would have gone. But what if it hadn't? 'She can't go walking up the road in her wedding dress. Why don't I go and get what she needs?'

'Since when did you start being so helpful?' Sandra snorted. 'I'm the bridesmaid, I'm meant to do that.'

'You're in your bridesmaid's dress. I could take Freddy with me, to give me a hand.'

'Oh,' she said. 'I see.'

She gave Freddy the key to their back door. Freddy put on a Bobby Darin LP and we walked up to Sandra and Marie's house. As we passed the shops he took my hand. Johnny's van was still outside the newsagent. Freddy squeezed my fingers tight.

'I don't care if she does love him,' he said, as if he could read my mind. 'That's all romantic crap. The bloke's a loser. He'd bring nothing but trouble to the house.'

Later, after Marie had changed her dress and her

shoes, and thrown the bouquet, which unfairly Deirdre caught, we all went into the car park. Bill and Marie were driving to Leigh-on-Sea where a friend of his mum's owned a caravan. Marie looked glamorous and different, in the tight shiny dress and jacket I had brought carefully from her wardrobe. She was even wearing a hat. The Mini was covered in tin cans and Crazy Foam. Bill shook his head and wanted to untie the tins. Marie put her hand on his arm. She was telling him to wait till they'd driven down the road. He put his arm round her and kissed the top of her head. She brushed a few stray pieces of confetti from his shoulder. I didn't know what to think.

Freddy had stayed inside to look after the music. The dramatic sounds of 'Runaway' floated into the open air. Del Shannon, my favourite. I wondered if he would dance with me again, once Bill and Marie were safely on their way and Sandra's mum and dad had stopped muttering and worrying.

Marie waved at everyone, a smile stretched right across her face. They climbed into the car and drove away down the road, away from the shops, away from the estate and away from Johnny Brown.

THE COCKTAIL PARTY

From the back seat of the car I said, 'Why have they asked you?' I looked at dad's trilby, soft and squashed with wear, at mum's formal suit making her sit uncomfortably. We were a stupid family that did not fit in.

'They are our friends, and you Linda will be polite and you will talk to people properly,' mum said.

'No-one's going to talk to me, they'll just think I'm a mod.'

'That will mean very little to the guests.'

'Snobs you mean, they'll all be snobs. And I'll probably end up stuck in some nursery room looking after those horrible horrible children.'

I slumped back in the corner of the car and smoothed my skirt. At least I would look neat.

The Grenvilles were friends of mum's from CND. Mrs Grenville was the Secretary and mum was the Treasurer. The Grenvilles were posh, like most of the people in CND, posher than us anyway. They lived in the middle of a field in the country and owned a pig farm. They had two children that I had baby sat once or twice.

The room was full of people. There was not a child in sight. We stood at the doorway, hearing languages that I could not identify. A lot of people were black. Some were Asian. Men wore open necked shirts, the women wore flowery dresses.

Mum gripped dad's arm. 'Harry! I'm overdressed,' she said.

'Just take your jacket off,' he murmured.

Mum casually slipped her jacket from her shoulders, dad loosened his tie and with similar nonchalance removed his own jacket. The three of us stood there, looking around. I wished we hadn't come. If I was here with Sandra, we'd have turned round and walked out straight away.

Mr Grenville came up with a big smile and two glasses of wine.

'Oh,' mum said. 'Not for me.' She was tee total.

'I'll have it,' I said.

'No you won't.'

Mr Grenville said, 'Come and choose your poison, Vera. We've got quite an array.' He and mum went over to the table of drinks.

'Harry!' A woman in an electric blue cocktail dress and bright red lipstick stalked up to dad. She was really overdressed. 'Come and meet Jonah Winston, he's in the African Studies department at UCL.'

Dad took a mouthful of wine and moved over to a group of people standing by the bookcase. He made a comment and everyone laughed at his joke.

For a moment I stared at dad, then I looked over at mum. In this room, they both looked different. Relaxed, happy. Now that she'd got over her wardrobe crisis mum was enjoying herself. She was smiling at something Mr Grenville was saying, then she said something back and he grinned and nodded.

Dad was lighting a cigarette and shaking his match slowly listening to something one of the older black men was saying, nodding his head in agreement.

But how was I going to get through this evening? No one was going to be interested in me. I walked over to the open window and perched on the arm of the settee looking out at the garden.

A man with curly brown hair and glasses came and stood beside me, also gazing out of the window. 'Do you think if you looked out on a vista like this every day it would affect the way you view the world?'

I looked round the room. He was talking to me. I opened my eyes wide. 'Well, it probably would, but it might make you a bit complacent.' I had never said the word complacent out loud.

'Interesting concept,' he said, still not looking at me. 'What do you mean?'

What did I mean? 'Well, mightn't it make you forget there's a world out there that hasn't got a vista like this?'

'Maybe.'

'What view do you have from your window?'

'That depends where I am.' He had a foreign accent, he pronounced the letter 'r' in the back of his throat and 'a' as 'e'. 'If I am in London, in my tiny flat' he said, flet, 'I have a view of other mansion blocks.'

'London,' I said.

'In Berlin I overlook a very busy street. There is not a tree to be seen. What do you see from your window?'

'In Chelmsford I see our shed and old people's bungalows at the end of the garden. And trees my dad plants. And that's it.'

'What is the view from the window in your imagination?'

I glanced at his face. Was this a joke? He was waiting. 'In my imagination, the view is … a sandy road, with scrubby trees, and a thin wire fence on one side that may be keeping wild animals at bay. And the sun is beating down.'

'Really?' he said. 'And what country do you live in, in your imagination?'

I shouldn't have started this. Where? 'Africa,' I said miserably. Africa was so big.

'And what are you doing in Africa?' he said.

'I'm –' I shook my head. 'I'm a journalist.'

'And what sort of stories do you write?'

Was he laughing at me? I looked at him. He was

gazing out of the window, smoking thoughtfully.

'I write about people's lives. The political situation. Racialism.'

'Well, depending on which country you actually go to –'

'Kenya, probably,' I said, wildly, hoping he wouldn't ask why, so that I wouldn't have to say it was because of the Tommy Steele song.

'Well,' he said, 'I don't know people in Nairobi, but if you are interested in journalism you could come to my country and work on a newspaper, there.'

'In Berlin? Germany?' I failed the exam, I didn't say.

He laughed. 'Yes! My friend edits an English language paper there. I could put you in touch with him. They need people like you.'

'What do you mean?'

He laughed. 'Young, energetic. Speakers of good English.'

'Which part of Berlin?' I said, hesitantly. East? West? I knew the difference.

'West Berlin but with interesting connections. You could report on that.'

The Grenvilles' front room was transformed. The

noise of conversation slid away. The bare walls and neutral colours became the calm backdrop to another world, a world of young radical people, some even with beards, intensely discussing politics and peace, in roughly painted rooms and I was mingling with them, joining the discussion, voicing an opinion, writing it down, transmitting it to the world.

My companion drew a flat packet of cigarettes from his trouser pocket. He offered it to me.

'I don't smoke,' I said.

'Do you mind if I ...?'

'No, please.'

He lit a match and inhaled deeply.

Together we looked out of the window in silence. But I wasn't looking at the view. I was listening to the room, the relaxed nature of the group, the gentle hum of conversation, the intermittent clink of glasses, the occasional roar of laughter. People saying words I wanted to hear, communism, South Africa, Bertrand Russell, Bernard Shaw. Words I'd only ever read in the books on our bookshelves at home. Black and white people being together in a room like they couldn't be in Johannesburg. I was watching myself sitting on the arm of a sofa talking to a man who was just talking, not posing, not trying, not doing anything, just talking, in a room with pale walls and big windows as the sun was setting. I liked being here. I was drinking it in.

'I'm Kai, by the way.'

'I'm Linda.' We shook hands.

He looked at me and smiled. 'Do you write already?'

'Just letters and things. My diary.' I felt stupid but free at the same time.

'You could write to my friend in Berlin. You don't even have to go there. Do a column for him.'

He was talking dreams. 'What would I write about? I live in Chelmsford. I live on a council estate.'

'That sounds intriguing.' He glanced at me. 'Writing for a newspaper is hard work. But you might like it. And then, come to Berlin – why not? After that, who knows? You could move on to Africa.'

I smiled. Here was someone who was taking me seriously. I wanted to keep talking about me, but I knew I should ask him questions. 'What do you do?'

'I'm an architect.'

'Is that why you're here?'

'Probably. I suppose I'm a friend of the

Grenvilles. Alice Grenville and I studied together. Why are you here?'

'I don't know. I think because of CND. And my dad.'

'The tree planter.'

'Yes, but I don't think trees are the reason. He's a trade unionist. People like that.'

'Do you like it?'

'Yes, I do.'

'Write about that.'

'Is that interesting?'

'Depends how you write it. You seem an interesting person, you could make it interesting.'

This was too nice. 'Are you saying I'm interesting just because I'm here at this party?'

'You're a cynic, perhaps?' The romance of his accent.

'Perhaps.' I felt a pang of guilt. I was so enjoying this conversation, and yet, I'd had conversations like this a million times with Sylvie, the unmarried mother who lived in the Crescent, who was considered dangerous by most people in our road, but I hadn't enjoyed them in the same way. Was that because we had conversations in her front room with nappies and copies of the Daily Mirror and no bookshelves and curtains that didn't fit the windows? 'I mean, I like it here, in this room, watching the sun go down and people here, foreign people, just talking, laughing, the cigarettes. But do I belong here?'

'Does any of us belong here? We are just passing through.'

'But I'm a mod.'

'What is that – I don't think I understand.'

'It's what you do if you're young and not a rocker. Mods and rockers?'

'Ahhhh.'

'But we're working class. So people don't think much about it, I mean except to say "They're fighting again". But the clothes are good.'

He laughed. 'Are these – eh - mod clothes that you are wearing?'

'They are, as it happens.' I looked down at my straight grey skirt.

'It's an interesting look. How would you describe it? Neat, functional?'

'Well ironed.' We laughed.

And then Mrs Grenville was there, saying, 'Linda, you speak French don't you?'

I looked at her, thrilled and astounded. Then

terrified. 'Well.'

'Your father says it's your favourite lesson.'

'Oh.' That was unexpected.

'Come and meet Leonard.' She pronounced it Lay Oh Nah. 'He's from the Ivory Coast and he's a little out of his depth.'

'I can't swim,' I said. I looked at my conversationalist but he had turned away. Had I bored him? Had he sent a sign to Mrs Grenville that he needed to be rescued?

Leonard was tall and thin. He had a very faint smell of fresh sweat which I realised I quite liked. We spoke lumberingly, clumsily.

He wasn't happy. 'Pourquoi je suis la?'

'Je ne sais pas.'

'Tous ces gens la, qu'est ce qu'ils savent de mon histoire?'

'Je ne sais pas.'

'You are just a girl. You know nothing.'

'I probably know more than you do about some things.' He didn't want to speak to me and I didn't want to speak to him, in any language.

'Like what?'

I didn't know. 'William Shakespeare.'

'Perhaps. I don't need to know about him. I am a

student of law.'

'What, in Chelmsford? I could tell you about the law in Chelmsford.' Sandra's boyfriend Danny appeared regularly in the magistrates' court.

'That could be interesting. Perhaps we could discuss this over a cup of your horrible English tea?'

'I'm a Socialist,' I said. 'You might not like that.'

A smile lit up his face. 'I like Socialists. Socialism is how people in Africa have lived for hundreds of years. I am interested that you do not call yourself a communist. Karl Marx was merely describing the system of financial exchange that my family have known since the beginning of time. You have a gap in your teeth, that's sexy,' he said.

'Oh don't you start.' His English wasn't that bad.

He laughed. A giant roar from his stomach. 'I like you. I will come to your house and meet your parents and sample some more of your wonderful English cooking.'

'Then you'd better not come,' I said. 'Unless you like egg on toast.'

'You could come to my digs,' he said. 'That woman there.' He pointed to the woman in the electric blue cocktail dress. 'She is my landlady. I will cook a very good meal for all of us. I will make a special trip to London for the ingredients.' I was tingling with pleasure. 'I will ask Mrs Grenville for your telephone number. And then you can help me with my legal studies. I am having a little trouble with your friend Archibold.'

'I've never met him,' I said. 'But he's probably all right when you get to know him.'

'It's a book,' he said. 'A big thick book.' He put his arm round me and gave me a loud kiss on the cheek.

As we were leaving, Kai my conversationalist came across. 'Here is my number. Ring me about Berlin.'

'I will,' I said. 'I'll ring you next week.'

Mum looked at me.

'Good,' he said. 'We can have lunch. You come to London, don't you?'

'Yes,' I said. 'Yes, I do.'

THE RETURN

Deirdre was in the garden doing the rounds of her new vegetable patch, stroking the leaves of the tomatoes, wondering as she did every year, that they could look like that, feathery, pale, dipping down and produce something so red, so round. It wasn't yet 8 o'clock and the air was still fresh. When the phone rang, she had a burst of anxiety. Catherine?

It was Marie.

She hadn't heard from Marie for a very long time. She hadn't even been invited to Marie's 40th. And here she was ringing at 8 o'clock on a Saturday morning. They went through the hellos and how-are-yous.

Then Marie said, 'Guess what. Mick's back in town.'

Deirdre couldn't speak.

Marie said, 'Deirdre? Hello? Hello? Are you there?'

Her heart was pounding and she couldn't swallow. 'Mick?' she said. 'Mick Flynn?' Her breath was coming in short bursts. 'My goodness.'

'He's been in the States,' she said, and Deirdre wanted to say, 'I knew that,' but she didn't. 'I got a phone call last night,' Marie said. 'I'm trying to get a group of people together to meet up in the Golden Fleece tonight. Jeff and those.' Even though she didn't live in Chelmsford any more Marie kept up with the old crowd. 'Do you fancy coming? The others have all said they'll be there.'

So Deirdre wasn't the first on her list. 'Well. Well, yes. Yes, I'll come,' she said.

'Hooray!' said Marie. 'At last.'

'What are you going to wear?'

'I don't know, something casual. Doesn't really matter, does it?' she said. 'He won't care.'

Deirdre put the phone down. Mick Flynn. Mick. She stared at the pale wispy tomato leaf between her fingers. It needed a stick to prop it up. She swallowed. Mick. Flynn. And now he's coming back, she thought, and jabbed a stick into the soil.

She was late, she couldn't find anywhere to park, all the spaces in her usual street were taken. She didn't often come out on a Saturday night. The pub was crowded, but the first thing she heard was Marie's laugh, high, light, attractive.

And there they all were, sitting in a group, Marie, Jeff, one or two of the others that Deirdre vaguely recognised. It was a shock to see them looking so much older, but their thinning hair was cut short, they were neat in Ben Sherman shirts and slacks, the timeless uniform. But Marie – how could she? She was wearing sophisticated make-up and a dark dress with sequins. And teetering high heels. She looked glamorous and sparkling. Deirdre could smell her heavy, French perfume. Why hadn't she said? Deirdre looked down at her outfit –she'd made an effort, in a way, she'd tried to recreate the old mod look – a straight skirt, a twin set from Marks and

Spencers, flat moccasins. It had been the style then, but now the joke fell flat. Deirdre saw herself, she looked dull and stupid.

And there was Mick, sitting right next to Marie. He was wearing light tinted glasses and a stylish dark suit. Typical Mick, keeping up with the fashion. But there was something else, with his light tan, and his legs elegantly crossed, he was sophisticated, urbane. No-one Deirdre knew.

As she hovered at the edge of the group Marie noticed her, looked her up and down, then said almost reluctantly, 'And here's Deirdre.'

Jeff said, 'Hullo Deirdre, how are you? Marie didn't say you were coming. What are you drinking? Rum and black like the old days?'

'Oh no,' Marie said. 'Deirdre doesn't drink anymore. Not since she came back from Lincoln, all those years ago.'

'Glass of milk then Deirdre?' Jeff said. He laughed.

'No, it's OK, I ...'

Marie said to Mick. 'Do you remember Deirdre, Mick?'

He turned his face.

Deirdre said, 'I used to wash my hair in Sarson's

vinegar.'

'Did you?' he said, politely.

There was a pause. 'Come on,' said Marie, 'We don't want to talk about salad dressing. We want to eat it. Let's go and find our table.'

Everyone stood up.

Deirdre was panicking. Eating? A table? She hadn't come for a meal. She'd only brought enough money for a round of drinks. She wasn't sure she'd even brought her cheque book. She couldn't sit here all evening knowing she couldn't pay, in these clothes, being polite to people she didn't know, not saying anything she really wanted to say.

'Actually, it's OK,' she said. 'I really just came to say hello.' She looked desperately round the group.

'You've only just got here,' Marie said.

'I've got to … got to go…'

'Where, where are you going on a Saturday?' Marie rolled her eyes.

'To the gym.'

'In that outfit?'

'I get changed. Anyway my car's parked badly. Lovely to see you all again.'

'If you're so worried about fitness, why didn't

you walk?' Marie said. 'Sit down. You know you want to. Jeff, order her a Pina Colada. You can have it with your meal. Pretend it's a fruit juice.'

Jeff stood up. 'That's a good look, Deirdre,' he said. 'You always knew how to look nice.'

'I taught her everything she knows,' Marie said.

'Well, I'm not sure about your definition of casual,' Deirdre said.

'This old thing?' Marie looked down at her dress. 'You should see me when I'm really dressed up.' She picked up her bag and stalked towards the restaurant. The others followed. Except Mick. He and Deirdre remained, standing alone.

'Just the two of us then,' Deirdre said. 'How did that happen?'

'Do I know you?' Mick said.

Deirdre coughed. 'Well, you did.'

'Did we … did we go out together?'

'Only for a bit.'

'I'm so sorry.' His voice was different. The Essex tones had gone. This voice was smooth, distinct. 'I just don't remember you. Talk to me. Sit down and talk to me.'

They sat down again and he put his hands loosely on his knees.

'It was after your accident. I didn't know you before.'

'You were lucky – I was wild then.'

'You were pretty furious when I knew you.'

He laughed.

'Marie and I came up to your house. We walked round town, we went down the Orpheus, we went to the Corn Exchange. I had a brown suede.'

'And Marie had a navy blue one. I remember you. You were a good dancer. And you lived somewhere in Broomfield.'

'We used to go home in a taxi. I'd never been in a taxi before.'

'But didn't we park outside some farm houses or something?'

'So my mum didn't come out and find us.'

'We never went into each other's houses, did we?' he said.

'Well, once. When you were 18 on your birthday, I came to your nan's house with a birthday cake.'

'On your own?' he asked, but it was almost a statement.

'Yes. Marie was going to come but she went to London with Bill.'

'I'm glad she didn't come,' he said.

What did he mean?

'The cake had candles, didn't it?' he said.

'I lit them.'

'But I couldn't blow them out.' His bent his head, frowning at the memory. 'I kept missing them. I went crazy. Didn't I throw the cake in the air?'

'Yes. I jumped on all the candles to stop them burning the carpet.'

He laughed, his head still bent. 'You kept saying you had to clear it up before my nan came home.'

'There was cream on the armchair,' Deirdre said. 'And a flower in the carpet got singed.' And my cardigan, she thought.

'I was so angry with you. With everything. I stormed off to my room.'

'And I –'

'You came in, after. There was a smell of burning.' It was her best cardigan.

'Do you want another drink?' Deirdre said. She started to get up.

'You were the first person I ever slept with,' he said.

'Was I?' She sat back down again. 'That's not what you said at the time.'

'I think I must have been rough. Oh god, sorry, tell me your name again?'

'Deirdre. You weren't rough, not after the first bit. It was my first time too.' And the last, she thought.

'Two virgins together,' he said. 'I was so clumsy.'

'No you weren't. You were soft, gentle. We kissed a lot.' You cried, she thought.

'You were so free.'

Because you were so blind she didn't say.

'I'm glad it was you.' He lifted his face. 'What happened to us?'

'Oh -' Deirdre looked round the room. '- I ... we ... drifted apart.'

'Are you all right? Were you all right then?'

She took a deep breath.

'Mick!' Marie was walking across the room. 'We're all in the dining room. The waiter wants to take your order.'

'Why did you come back?' Deirdre said desperately.

Marie walked up to Mick. He gave a slight jump as she slid her arm round his neck, but his expression didn't change.

'Sorry,' Marie said. 'We forgot you.'

'No you didn't, we were talking,' Mick said. 'Catching up.'

Deirdre looked at his face. Seeing her reflection in his glasses was like seeing Catherine, the different parts of her, Deirdre, him. The urge to tell him was like clotted cream in her mouth.

'This is great,' Marie said. 'I've booked a table for eight and there's only me and those three in there. Jeff's disappeared, you two are here. I don't know why I bother. You might as well go to the gym, Deirdre. This evening is a fiasco.'

Deirdre sat up very straight.

'No don't go,' Mick said. His hand found her knee. 'What material's this?'

'It's pin-stripe,' she said.

'Were you the one with the grey pin-striped skirt?'

'Oh for god's sake,' Marie said. She stepped backwards. 'If you want to take part in this get-together I shall be next door, getting together with Barry and Dave and Norm, and possibly Jeff if he can ever find someone to serve him at the bar.'

Deirdre watched her retreat to the dining room.

'I came back because – well, the main reason, this

time, is my mum dying.'

'I'm sorry.' This time? He'd been back before. He'd been here and she didn't know.

'She was old. But then, I thought I'd see if there was anyone in Chelmsford who remembered me.'

'I don't think there's any question about that.'

'But not always for the right reasons.'

'You were our hero.'

'Not to everyone.'

'You mean the rocker?'

'No.' He suddenly raised his head. 'It was you, wasn't it?'

'What? What do you mean "it was me"?'

'You have kids?'

'One.'

'Yes, Marie wrote and told me. What's her name? Your daughter. Catherine?'

'Catherine. But what do you mean? Marie didn't know.'

'You two were best friends, weren't you?

'At one time.'

'She wrote me a letter about it. I think she was a bit jealous.'

'What?'

'Her tone was a bit sharper than usual, I seem to

recall.'

'But why was she telling you?' Her heart was pounding. 'Did she, did Marie say anything else?'

'It was a long time ago. She usually says we all ought to stay in touch. Yeah, that was probably the letter where she said she didn't see enough of you. She missed you. Especially after Bill went off.'

'Did she say anything about the – em – the father?'

'The father? What about him?' He paused.

Marie appeared in the doorway. She made a questioning face at Deirdre. Deirdre wondered how she had known. She must have guessed, at the fitting for the bridesmaid's dress perhaps, Deirdre's body still plump from the pregnancy, or simply from counting backwards after meeting Catherine. She wondered if Marie really had been jealous, or was she only being protective of her, trying to nudge Mick into taking responsibility? Had she really missed her? Deirdre had missed Marie. She wondered why Marie had asked her to come tonight.

'But you know, I'd like to keep in touch,' Mick was saying. 'Perhaps while I'm here we can go out together. Maybe meet Catherine. If that would be OK.'

What did he know? Deirdre thought. What had Marie actually told him?

The expression on Marie's face changed from curious to concerned and she beckoned to Deirdre. Deirdre smiled at her.

'Shall we go and have something to eat, Mick?' Deirdre said. 'But I warn you, I've got no money.'

'Oh Mick can pay,' Marie said, across the room. 'It's the least he can do.'

Deirdre stood up, linked her arm through his and they walked to the restaurant.

PRAISE FOR ELIZABETH WOODCRAFT

Good Bad Woman

'… sparklingly written, with believable dialogue and a lively plot.' Marcel Berlins, *the Guardian*

'My current favourite is debut author Elizabeth Woodcraft … funny, engaging.' *The Bookseller*

'She has a record collection worthy of any of the characters from High Fidelity.' *Evening Herald*, Dublin

'Hip, funny and a strong female character.' *Murder One*

'Sharp, streetwise and engaging.' *Western Mail*

'.. unusual and compelling … with the bonus of a Motown soundtrack.' *Time Out*

'Frankie Richmond is a great creation - more please.' Cath Staincliffe, *Manchester Evening News*

Babyface

'Elizabeth Woodcraft has created in Richmond the sort of lawyer that we want to side with, … in touch, switched on and with a life. Move over Rumpole.' The Times

'Unusual and highly readable' Shots magazine

'Witty and well-plotted this is a funny, action-packed legal thriller.' Birmingham Sunday Mercury

'The plot is clever and racy ... Richmond is lively and self-deprecatingly funny, and the frenetic, unreal atmosphere of the bar is portrayed with authenticity and wit.' Marcel Berlins, the Guardian

'...a belt-it-out Motown woman.' Ireland on Sunday

29812668R00072

Printed in Great Britain
by Amazon